A HARE, A HOUND
& SHY MOUSEY BROWN

To the ones who make me jump for joy –
Mark, James, Joe and Jess—JH

For Madison, Dakota, Bailey and Cooper—JB

Little Hare Books
an imprint of
Hardie Grant Egmont
Ground Floor, Building 1, 658 Church Street
Richmond, VIC 3121, Australia

www.littleharebooks.com

Text copyright © Julia Hubery 2012
Illustrations copyright © Jonathan Bentley 2012

First published 2012

Cataloguing-in-Publication details are available from the National Library of Australia

ISBN 978 1 921541 38 4 (hbk.)

Designed by Vida & Luke Kelly
Produced by Pica Digital, Singapore
Printed through Phoenix Offset
Printed in Shen Zhen, Guangdong Province, China, June 2012

5 4 3 2 1

Julia Hubery &
Jonathan Bentley

A Hare a Hound &

Shy
Mousey
Brown

LITTLE HARE
www.littleharebooks.com

There's a hare in the air, there's a hound on the ground,
and watching them both is shy Mousey Brown
from his hole in the wall, not making a sound,
so nobody knows that he's there.

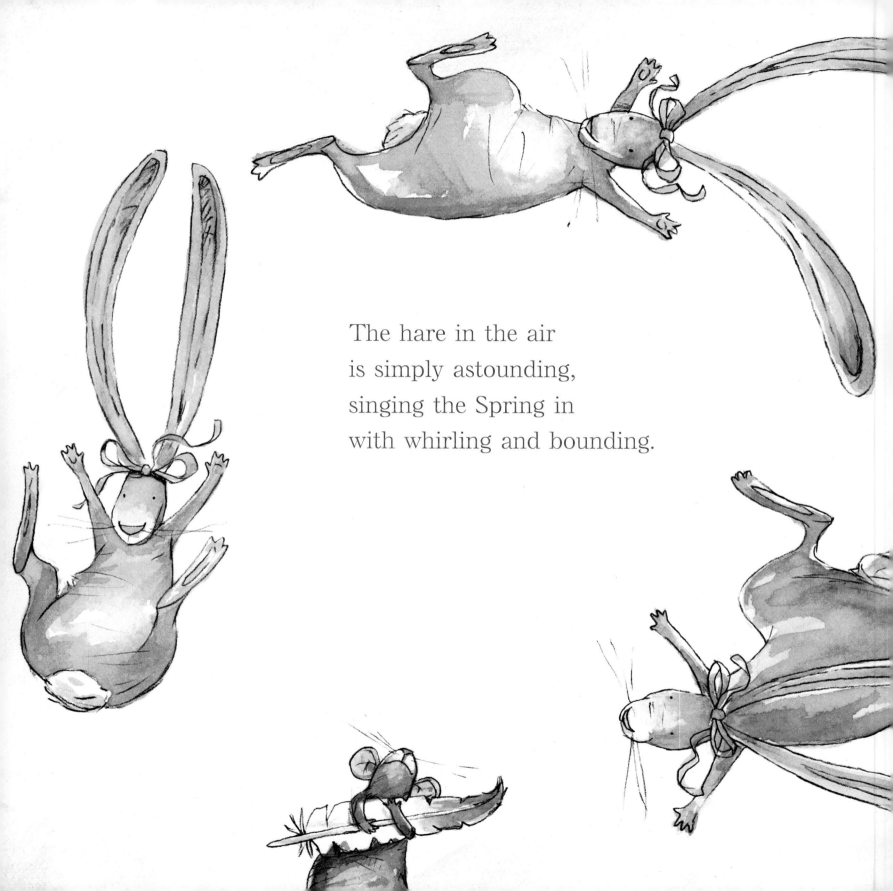

The hare in the air
is simply astounding,
singing the Spring in
with whirling and bounding.

Mousey Brown's heart
goes pitter-pat-pounding
with love for her daring and flair.

Wondrously *wild*, and fearlessly *free*,

she jumps for the *joy* of just being *she*.

"How could I hope
that she'd even see me?"
thinks poor Mousey Brown
in despair.

The daft dizzy dancer goes
laughing and leaping
right up to the hound,
who pretends to be sleeping,

but Mousey Brown knows
that he's secretly keeping
a watch on the hoppity hare.

For he knows this sly dog, he's seen him before:
he'll lie there as still as a log till he's sure
that the hare is in reach of his snappity jaws—
then he'll snatch her right out of the air!

"How can I warn her? I'm so very small!"
thinks shy Mousey Brown in his hole in the wall.

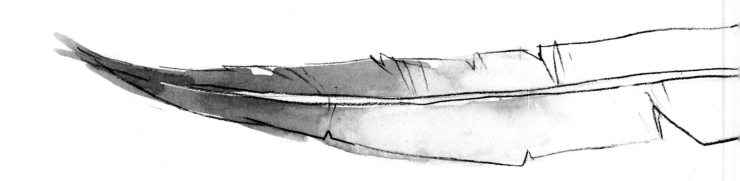

He takes a deep breath, and he leans out and bawls in his biggest best bellow:

"Bewa

But the hare doesn't hear him,
she pats the hound's nose,
tweaks his old tail, and tickles his toes.

"Wake up, sleepy doggy,
   it's springtime, you knows!"
she whispers right into his ear.

With a

leap
and a **snap**
and a *swipe* of his paw,
the hound on the ground
isn't there any more.
He's up in the air
and he's boxing the hare …

with a ***thud!***

and a ***thwack!***

she's pinned on her back,
and quakes at his menacing stare.

Her beautiful eyes are shining with fear
as he lashes a lick up her long lovely ear.
"Gosh, you'll be ever so tasty!" he sneers …

and Mousey Brown
leaps from his lair!

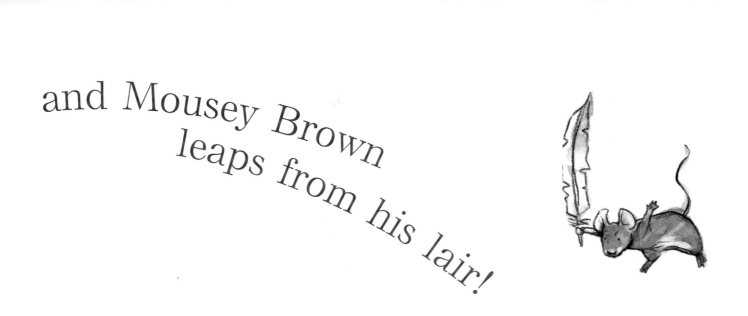

Clutching a feather, he hurls himself down
right into the ear of the huge hungry hound

and relentlessly *tickles*,
the hound into *giggles*,

wriggles

until he's wound tight in a knot with his

and can't move a whisker or hair.

Then Mousey strides out
with his feather held high,
he feels like a warrior,
tall as the sky.

He bows to the hare
with a bold twinkling eye,
and says, "Pleased to meet you,
my dear!"

"You saved me!"
the hare cries.
"I'll love you forever
you bold mouseketeer,
so fearless and clever!

Come with me now,
let's go dancing together,
we've got a whole springtime
to share!"

Mousey Brown and the hare
make a curious pair,
and when they go dancing,
the neighbours all stare.

The hare doesn't notice,
Mousey Brown doesn't care ...

and they'll never be parted—so there!